There's a WOCKET in my POCKET!

By Dr. Seuss

HarperCollins *Children's Books*

And a
FINDOW
in my
WINDOW

The Cat in the Hat
™ & © Dr. Seuss Enterprises, L.P. 1957
All Rights Reserved

ISBN-13: 978-0-00-789238-9

© 1974, 2002 by Dr. Seuss Enterprises, L.P.
All Rights Reserved
A Bright and Early Book for Beginning Beginners,
published by arrangement with Random House Inc.,
New York, USA
First published in the UK 1975
This edition published in the UK 2010 by
HarperCollins*Children's Books,*
a division of HarperCollins*Publishers* Ltd
77-85 Fulham Palace Road
London W6 8JB

Visit our website at:
www.harpercollins.co.uk

Printed and bound in Thailand

Did you
ever have the feeling
there's a
WASKET
in your
BASKET?

. . . Or a NUREAU
in your BUREAU?

... Or a WOSET in your CLOSET?

Sometimes
I feel quite CERTAIN
there's a JERTAIN
in the CURTAIN.

Sometimes
I have the feeling
there's a ZLOCK
behind the CLOCK.

And that ZELF
up on that SHELF!

I have
talked to him
myself.

That's the
kind of house
I live in.

There's a NINK
in the SINK.

And a
ZAMP
in the
LAMP.

And they're
rather nice
. . . I think.

Some of them
are very friendly.

Like the
YOT
in the
POT.

But
that
YOTTLE
in
the
BOTTLE!

Some are friendly.
Some are NOT.

I like the
ZABLE
on the
TABLE.

And the
GHAIR under the CHAIR.

But that BOFA
  on the SOFA...

Well,
I wish
he wasn't there.

All those NUPBOARDS
in the CUPBOARDS.

They're good fun
to have about.

But that
NOOTH GRUSH
on my
TOOTH BRUSH...

Him
I could
do without!

The only one
I'm really scared of
is   that   VUG
under the RUG.

And that QUIMNEY
up the CHIMNEY . . .

I don't like him.
Not at all.

And it makes me sort of nervous
when the ZALL scoots down the HALL.

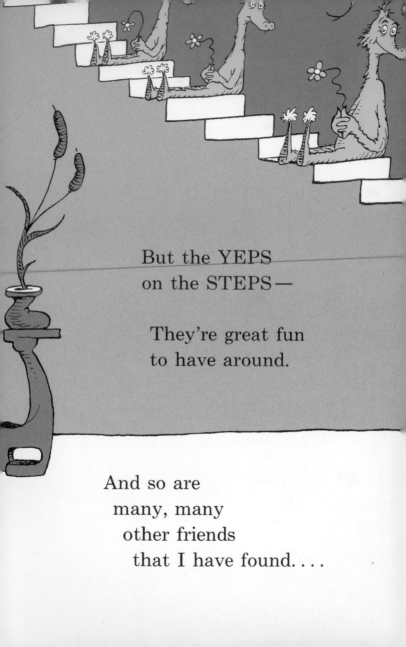

But the YEPS
on the STEPS—

They're great fun
to have around.

And so are
many, many
other friends
that I have found. . . .

. . . Like the TELLAR
and the NELLAR
and the GELLAR
and the DELLAR
and the BELLAR
and the WELLAR
and the ZELLAR
in the CELLAR

. . . And the GEELING
on the CEILING . . .

... and
the
ZOWER
in
my
SHOWER ...

. . . and the ZILLOW
    on my PILLOW.

        I don't care
        if you believe it.
        That's the kind of house
        I live in.
        And I hope
        we never leave it.